JUST A MESS

BY
MERCER MAYER

A Random House PICTUREBACK® Book

Random House 🏠 New York

www.randomhouse.com/kids
Educators and librarians, for a variety of teaching tools, visit us at
www.randomhouse.com/teachers
Library of Congress Control Number: 86-82369
ISBN-13: 978-0-307-11948-3   ISBN-10: 0-307-11948-3
Printed in the United States of America
23 22 21 20 19
First Random House Edition 2006

Today I couldn't find my baseball mitt.

I looked in my tree house.

I looked under the back steps.

I asked Mom if she had seen it.
She said I should try my room.

I never thought to look there.
What a mess!

Mom said it was time
to clean my room.
So I asked her to help.

She said, "You made the mess,
so you can clean up the mess."

Dad was working in the yard.
He said he was too busy to help me.

My little sister said, "No way!"
And the baby didn't understand.

I just did it myself.

First, I put a few things in the closet.

I put my clothes
in the drawers.

I straightened up
my games.

shut the lid
to my toy box

and put away my books.

The rest of the mess could fit under my bed,
so I put it there.

Then I made the bed.
Won't Mom be pleased.

I thought I might wash the floor.

But Mom said, "NO!"
So I just vacuumed instead.

Everything was just about perfect.

Then I noticed that my pillow was missing.

I looked on the other side of my bed,

and guess what I found?

My baseball mitt.